Princess Poppy
Pocket Money Princess

Check out Princess Poppy's website
to find out all about the other
books in the series

www.princesspoppy.com

Princess Poppy
Pocket Money
Princess

written by Janey Louise Jones
Illustrated by Samantha Chaffey

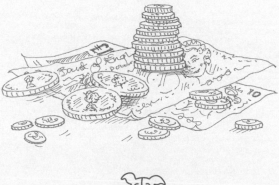

POCKET MONEY PRINCESS
A YOUNG CORGI BOOK 978 0 552 55857 0

First published in Great Britain by Young Corgi,
an imprint of Random House Children's Books
A Random House Group Company

Young Corgi edition published 2007
This Young Corgi edition, with CD, published 2008

1 3 5 7 9 10 8 6 4 2

Set in 14/21pt Bembo MT Schoolbook
by Falcon Oast Graphics Art Ltd.

Young Corgi are published by Random House Children's Books,
61–63 Uxbridge Road, London W5 5SA

THE RANDOM HOUSE GROUP Limited Reg. No. 954009
www.kidsatrandomhouse.co.uk
www.princesspoppy.com

A CIP catalogue record for this book is available
from the British Library.

Printed and bound in China

For Nhan, our friend in Vietnam,
who would also love a shiny new bike

Honeypot Hill

Saffron Thimble's sewing shop

To the City

The Orchards

Paddle Steamer Quay

Ho
B

Lavender Valley Garden Centre

Healing House & Garden

The Worthington's House

Aun

Lavender Lake

Melody Maker's Music Shop

Lavender Lake School of Dance

Bumble Bee's Teashop

Hedgerows Hotel (where Mimosa lives)

SCHOOL

Peppermint Pond

Rosehip School

Summer Meadow

Christmas Corner

Wildspice Wood

Chapter One

Poppy was standing with Grandpa at the ticket office of the train station in Honeypot Hill.

"One adult and one child for Camomile Cove, please," Grandpa said to the ticket inspector just as the train pulled up. They climbed on and set off for the seaside.

Poppy was really excited to be going to Camomile Cove to visit her cousin Daisy – she hadn't seen her for absolutely ages. Grandpa was looking forward to it too because Daisy was always so busy with her friends and her part-time jobs these days that he hardly ever got to see his granddaughter either – not that she was terribly interested in seeing her old grandpa any more!

When they arrived at Shellbay House, where Daisy and her family lived, Poppy could hardly wait to hear all her cousin's news. Poppy thought Daisy's life was amazingly interesting compared to her own.

"Hi, Poppy," called Daisy. "Come on down to the summer house."

"Don't I get a kiss?" said Grandpa to his newly teenage granddaughter.

"Gramps! I don't do kisses any more," laughed Daisy as she led Poppy down the big garden towards the sea.

At the end of the long leafy garden was Daisy's summer house, nestling among tall summer flowers. The little wooden house was slightly raised from the ground and had steps

up to the front door; from inside there was a beautiful view out to sea and along the sandy beach.

"This is so cool. It's like having your own private house, Daisy. You are so lucky!" exclaimed Poppy.

"Yeah, I know. Isn't it fab? Me and my friends Lily and Rose spent the whole of last summer working in here to make it like this.

It was filthy before and full of junk. We cleaned it out and painted and decorated it ourselves – the inside and the outside. It was really hard work, but definitely worth it – it's such a great place to hang out."

Poppy gazed admiringly at her surroundings. Daisy had so many cool things in the summer house. She'd won masses of competitions on her pony, Parsley, and had pinned all her colourful rosettes on one wall in neat rows. There was a stereo, stacks of CDs and a microphone, posters of pop stars, lots of coloured folders, roller blades, handbags, jewellery and pretty little trinkets. Then Poppy noticed that there were loads of instruments: a drum kit, a keyboard, two guitars and a pile of tambourines, triangles, maracas and other shakers.

"Wow! Can you play *all* these instruments, Daisy?" asked Poppy.

"Well, we've just started a band. I play the

drums; my best friend Lily plays guitar; my
other best friend, Rose, plays the keyboard
and we all sing. We don't have anyone doing
backing vocals yet," explained Daisy, "but we
will soon."

"What's your band called?" asked Poppy,

5

desperate to hear more about it.

"The Beach Babes," replied Daisy. "We started it last summer and we're getting better and better all the time. We've got about four original songs and we're always working on new ones. At the moment we're practising for the end-of-term competition in two weeks' time. We're going to play one of our new songs. Some of the boys at school are in a rock band called Caves 'n' Rocks and they'll be playing too. Everyone at school has to vote for the band they think is the best! We *have* to win the vote and beat the boys!"

"Do you think you'll be famous?" asked Poppy. "That would be amazing!"

"That would be really cool," agreed Daisy, "but right now we're just trying to raise money for charity, although if we *were* famous, we'd be able to raise even more money."

Then Poppy noticed a gleaming new

mountain bike propped up against the
back wall.

"Wow, what an amazing bike. I love it!"
she said. "When did you get it?"

"Oh, a couple of months ago," Daisy
replied. "Mum, Dad and Edward gave me
half of it for my birthday but I had to pay
for the other half out of my earnings. We
bought it in Cycle Services in the City. It's
the coolest shop, with every sort of bike you
could ever imagine – it was really hard to
choose."

"Can I have a go on it?" asked Poppy.

"Yes, of course you can, but I think it's
probably a bit too big for you."

Just as she was wheeling the bike out of

the door, Poppy noticed a rather interesting-looking poster.

BARBECUE AND BEACH PARTY
Smuggler's Cove High School's
End of term bash!
MEET AT SANDY BAY FOR
A DAY YOU'LL NEVER
FORGET!

As soon as she read the poster, Poppy wanted to hear all about the party – it sounded so much fun.

"There's a big beach barbecue in two weeks for all the kids from Smuggler's Cove High School," explained Daisy. "The Battle of the Bands is on the same day, and after the show everyone goes for a bike ride through the woods and back to the beach for the barbecue. It's the best night of the year!"

"We never do things like that at my school!" complained Poppy. "We've just had an end-of-term picnic at Cornsilk Castle, but it wasn't nearly as cool as what you're doing!"

"A picnic sounds lovely," said Daisy. "Anyway, you'll get to do all these things when you're my age."

Poppy hoped so, but she wasn't so sure it was true. And anyway, she wanted to do them now.

Out in the garden, Daisy held her bike steady and helped Poppy to get onto it. Poppy was very shaky at first, but soon she was cycling the whole length of the garden even though the bike was far too big for her.

"Look at me, Grandpa!" she called as she wobbled past.

"Watch you don't fall now!" called Grandpa.

Poppy rolled her eyes – Grandpa treated

her like a complete baby.

"Do you want to come into Camomile Cove with me now? We can have a look at the shops and go for an ice cream at the Lighthouse Café. I'm meeting Rose there today," called Daisy as Poppy cycled back towards the summer house.

"Yes please, but I'd better just ask Grandpa if I'm allowed," said Poppy with a sigh.

Grandpa said they could go. "But if you're not back by two, I'll come along to the Lighthouse Café and disco dance in front of all your friends!"

"I promise we won't be late, Grandpa," said Poppy, delighted that she'd been allowed to go.

"Grandpa is sooooooooo embarrassing," Daisy whispered to her cousin. "We mustn't be late!"

Poppy had never really thought this before. She loved spending time with Grandpa, but if

Daisy thought he was embarrassing, then it must be true because Daisy was totally cool and was right about pretty much everything.

Before they left for the café, Daisy brushed her hair and put on some strawberry lip balm.

"Can I have some?" asked Poppy.

"Of course you can," smiled Daisy. "In fact, I've got a spare grape lip balm. You can have it if you like."

"Wow! Thanks!" beamed Poppy as she smeared the lip balm onto her lips and flicked her long hair, just like Daisy had a few moments before. The girls checked their shiny lips in front of the mirror and then set off for town.

Chapter Two

As they walked, the two girls chatted non-stop. Daisy asked Poppy all about her life and what she liked doing with her time, and then she told Poppy all about her friends, her school, the boys she liked, her jobs and what sort of music she listened to. The more Poppy heard about Daisy, the more she wanted to live the same kind of life. Everything Daisy did and liked seemed so cool and everything Poppy did just seemed babyish now, even though that morning she had been completely content with her lot! Poppy even started to feel a bit shy – she was sure Daisy wasn't really interested in what she got up to.

Daisy suddenly stopped chatting and pointed across the street to a very pretty girl who looked a couple of years older than her.

"See over there? That's Lilac Farrington. She's the coolest, prettiest girl at my school and she only hangs out with really cool girls. Me, Lily and Rose desperately want to be part of their group."

"But you *are* really cool!" said Poppy.

"We're not cool enough yet!" said Daisy. "But if the Beach Babes beat Caves 'n' Rocks, I'll definitely be as cool as Lilac Farrington and maybe she'll even come and hang out in the summer house with us!"

After Lilac had passed them, Poppy and Daisy crossed the road to look in the window of a boutique called Bijou. There were so many fabulous clothes, shoes and accessories — it was even better than Saffron's shop in Honeypot Hill!

"Lilac buys loads of her clothes here," Daisy told Poppy. "Shall we pop in and have a look around?"

Inside the shop there were so many things that Poppy wanted but she didn't have enough money. All she had was the coins Grandpa had given her for an ice-cream at the Lighthouse Café. She wished with all her heart that she had her own money so she could just buy whatever she liked. Poppy was fed up with Mum buying all her clothes for her.

Daisy picked out some T-shirts and went off to the changing room to try them on. Each time she put on a different one she came out to show Poppy.

"Which one do you think I should get?" she asked when she'd tried them all on.

"They all look really nice on you but my favourite is the purple one," said Poppy. "Have you got enough money to buy it?"

"I got paid yesterday for grooming all the horses at the stables, so actually I'll even have a bit of money left over after I've bought this," Daisy explained. "Would you like a necklace or something?"

Poppy's eyes lit up. "Yes, please!"

She picked out a pretty red flower necklace and Daisy fastened it around her neck.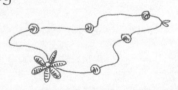

"This one really suits you. I'll pay for it and then we should go. Rose will be wondering where we've got to. Plus we don't have that much time – I really don't want Grandpa to turn up at the Lighthouse Café. That would be so embarrassing."

The Lighthouse Café was an old white-painted lighthouse at the end of the pier with a pale brick extension to one side. It was decorated inside with a seaside theme – the walls were pale blue and the floor was a golden sandy colour. All around there were shells and fishing creels, as well as interesting things that had been washed up on the beach: pieces of pottery, glass bottles and pretty pebbles.

Poppy felt so grown up but ever so slightly nervous as she sat down with Daisy and her friend Rose. She had never been to a café without an adult before – Bumble Bee's Teashop didn't count because Granny Bumble was always there and Mum would order the food and drinks and do all the speaking; Poppy wasn't really sure she knew what to say to the waitress. But there was no need to worry. The waitress came over and Daisy ordered chocolate fudge ice-cream sundaes for all of them. While they waited for the food to come, Daisy and Rose chatted away about shopping, hair, nails, make-up, music, boys, parties and clothes. It wasn't until they got onto the subject of ponies that Poppy felt able to join in the conversation – she knew so little about all the other things.

"That reminds me," she said. "Twinkletoes' fringe is getting in his eyes. I really should

braid it tomorrow or he won't be able to see a thing!"

"We braided Parsley's mane and tail for the last gymkhana – he looked so smart, didn't he, Rose?"

"He looked great. I just wish my pony's mane was long enough to braid, but I don't think it ever will be – it's always been short and tufty!" Rose replied.

"Maybe he needs some special grow-more shampoo for it!" joked Daisy. "I bet they sell it at Ned's – they sell everything there."

She turned to Poppy and told her all about Ned's, the saddler's shop in Camomile Cove.

"It's the most amazing shop. They've got *the* most fabulous pony accessories. I got a gorgeous pink halter there for Parsley and Rose got a blue one for her pony. Next time you come over we can go and have a look if you like."

The girls settled down to eat their delicious-looking sundaes – there was no more time for chatting! When they'd finished their food, Daisy looked up at the clock to check they were still all right for time.

"Poppy, we'd better go now or Grandpa will come to collect you and it will be soooooooooo cringeworthy – what if he tries to kiss me hello again?"

They said goodbye to Rose and headed back to Daisy's house.

When they got back, Daisy's friend Lily was in the kitchen chatting to Poppy's Aunt Delphi and Uncle Daniel – Daisy's mum and dad – and to Grandpa. Her brand-new bright red mountain bike was leaning against the house, just by the back door. Lily was slightly taller than Daisy and her red hair was cut into a sleek bob. She was wearing white shorts, a green vest top and matching green flip-flops – Poppy thought Lily looked great; she wished she had clothes like that.

"Hi!" smiled Lily as Daisy and Poppy walked into the kitchen. "You girls must have been shopping. What's in the bag?"

"Oh, I bought a new top," explained Daisy as she showed her friend the purple T-shirt she'd bought earlier.

"Nice! Is it from Bijou?" Lily enquired. "I think Lilac Farrington's got one like that but in yellow. Cool."

"Yep," replied Daisy. "They've got some lovely stuff there at the moment. I bought Poppy this necklace too."

"It looks really pretty, Poppy," smiled Lily. "I came over to see whether you were up for a beach party sleepover tomorrow night, Daisy. I'm trying to organize everything now."

Daisy looked at her mum. "Can I go? Pleeeease, Mum."

"Will there be any adults there?" asked her mum.

"Well, my dad is going to camp about a hundred metres along from us. I won't let him come any closer because he's really embarrassing and his snoring is super-bad," explained Lily.

"Oh, all right then," said Daisy's mum. "So long as you find your sleeping bag yourself, pack your own bag and it doesn't cost me anything!"

"Thanks, Mum, and don't worry, I've still got some of my wages left," smiled Daisy, delighted that she was allowed to go.

Poppy looked on in amazement. "You are so lucky, Daisy! You're allowed to do anything. Mum and Dad would never let me go to a camping sleepover like that. It's so unfair. My life is really boring," she moaned.

"Oh, Poppy, don't worry!" said Daisy. "I was never allowed to do stuff like this when I was your age either, but now Mum lets me because she thinks I'm grown up enough – you will be soon too."

Poppy thought she was grown up enough now. The only thing she lacked was money.

"Come on, Poppy!" said Grandpa. "It's high time we got back to Honeypot Hill. If we catch the next train, we'll have time to go to the adventure playground before supper."

Poppy's face went bright red. "Grandpa!

I don't like playing there any more; let's go and see Twinkletoes instead," she said, looking at Daisy and Lily and finding it hard to imagine either of them ever wanting to go and play at an adventure playground.

Just as Poppy and Grandpa were leaving, Daisy's little brother Edward burst in through the door.

"Hi, Princess Bossy Boots!" he said. "Been dressing up in any fancy tiaras lately?"

Poppy bit her bottom lip. She desperately wanted to be more grown up, but what hope was there with relations like Edward? They might have been the same age, but as far as Poppy was concerned, he was years younger – he behaved like such a baby.

Daisy smiled at her younger cousin, remembering how much fun she had had when she was Poppy's age. There was no need for Poppy to be ashamed at all. "We still love dressing up, don't we, Lily?"

Poppy smiled gratefully. "Come on, Grandpa, we've got to go now."

She said goodbye to Daisy and Lily and watched as the older girls jumped on their bikes and cycled into the distance. She would have absolutely loved to join them, but Mum and Dad wouldn't even let her come to Camomile Cove without an adult, let alone go on a bike ride with her older cousin.

Chapter Three

When Poppy and Grandpa got back to
Honeypot Hill, they decided to pop into
Riverside Stables to see how Poppy's pony
Twinkletoes was getting on.

"Daisy says there's a really good saddler's
shop in Camomile Cove. It's called Ned's
and she's promised to take me there next
time I go to see her. I can't wait," Poppy told
Grandpa as they walked to the stables
together. "Daisy bought a gorgeous pink
halter for Parsley there and Rose bought a

blue one for her pony. I think Twinks would look really nice in a red one. And I need a new grooming kit for him," she went on, hardly even pausing for breath. "And when I've got all that new stuff for him, I want to start taking part in gymkhanas, just like Daisy and Rose do. I'll need some new riding clothes before I can do that though."

Grandpa looked at his granddaughter kindly. "Poppy, it's not smart new riding clothes and pretty red halters that help you win shows; it's practice and hard work. Daisy's been riding for years, darling. That's why she's got so many rosettes. And all these things cost lots of money."

Humph! thought Poppy. *Why do adults always have to be so boring?*

Later, when Grandpa and Poppy got back to Honeysuckle Cottage, they found Mum in the kitchen. She was very busy clearing out all the cupboards. There were empty jam

jars, vases, pots, ornaments and old saucepans
everywhere. She had made a terrible mess
and was looking very hot and tired.

"What are you doing?" asked Poppy.

"It's the Cornsilk Castle car boot sale next
Sunday and I thought it was a good excuse
for a clear out. I'm going through the
cupboards to see whether there's anything
we don't need any more," explained Mum.

"It all looks like junk to me! Who would
buy it?" asked Poppy.

"One person's junk is another person's
treasure," smiled Mum and carried on with
what she was doing. "Why don't you help

prepare the vegetables? I've left some carrots and potatoes on the table for you to chop for tomorrow's soup," said Mum, "and you can tell me all about your day."

Poppy settled down at the kitchen table and started preparing the vegetables, chatting away at the same time and telling Mum what an amazing time she'd had at Camomile Cove.

"Mum, can I get a new bike?" she asked after she'd finished telling Mum all about Daisy's bike.

"But there's nothing wrong with the bike you've got," said Mum.

"Apart from the basket on the front and the silly stickers on the frame!" said Poppy. "My bike is really babyish. I need one like Daisy's – it's so cool."

Mum sighed.

"And I need some new clothes," Poppy went on. "I'm so embarrassed by all my clothes! Look at this babyish dress – Daisy would never wear something like this – all her clothes are soooooooooo much better. And I need a new haircut. Daisy has had layers cut into hers and she says that they give it more movement. Can I have layers cut into mine too?"

"Poppy, your hair is beautiful and you've got masses of lovely clothes. Anyway, where did you get that necklace?" asked Mum.

"Daisy bought it for me with her *own* money. She's so lucky – she can just go into a shop and buy whatever she wants, and Aunt Delphi lets her do whatever she wants too."

"Daisy has part-time jobs to earn extra money so that she can buy things for herself. Don't forget that she is quite a lot older than you. Daisy didn't have a job when she was your age," Mum explained.

Poppy was sure that Mum wasn't telling her the whole story, but she had a theory of her own. If she had her own money, she would be able to buy whatever she liked whenever she liked, and do whatever she liked too – just like Daisy. Poppy hadn't understood that the main issue wasn't money, it was her age. She was younger than Daisy and that was that. In time, Mum and Dad would let her do all the same things – get jobs, hang out with her friends, go on bike rides without an adult, have sleepovers – as soon as they thought she was ready.

"Can I see my bank book please?" Poppy asked her mum. "You always put my birthday money in the bank so there must be loads in there – definitely enough for a new bike. I think we should just put all the money in my dressing-table drawer and then I would be able to take money out whenever I need it without asking anyone."

Mum was getting quite cross with Poppy now. "And what will you do when you've spent all the savings on bikes and clothes and haircuts?" she asked as she started to clear a space so that she could cook supper.

"You can just give me more money," Poppy replied.

"It isn't as simple as that. Dad and I don't have an endless supply of money. We both work

31

hard to earn enough to live on and have some left over for the odd treat. We can't buy everything *we* want either – we have to make a budget and stick to it," Mum explained, but Poppy wasn't really listening any more. Mum was being as boring and sensible as Grandpa. She just didn't understand.

Mum sighed – Poppy was becoming a real handful. Perhaps her trip to Camomile Cove hadn't been a good idea after all. She didn't want Poppy to grow up too fast – she felt sure she was going to hear a lot more about Daisy, money and the bike!

"Can I go and see Honey?" said Poppy, checking her hair in the hall mirror as she passed it.

"All right, but don't be too long. Supper will be ready soon," replied Mum.

Poppy rang the doorbell of Honeypot Cottage – Honey was at the door in a flash.

"Hi, Poppy, come in," she said. "Wow! I love that necklace. Where did you get it?"

"Daisy bought it for me at a really cool boutique called Bijou. I went to Camomile Cove today and I had the best time. Daisy has a cool new bike and . . ." explained Poppy breathlessly. Then she told Honey all about her trip into town and her visit to the café; about Daisy's friends, the sleepover and all the wonderful shops her cousin had told her about.

"I wish we could go over to Camomile Cove on the train without an adult and just hang out with Daisy and Lily and Rose," Poppy moaned.

"Granny would never let me do that and it would take me ages to save up enough pocket money for the train fare!" Honey pointed out sensibly.

"Exactly! But if we had enough money of our *own*, we could do whatever we wanted," declared Poppy triumphantly.

"Yeah, I suppose so," said Honey. "I hadn't thought about it like that before. It would be really nice if I could buy my own clothes. Some of the things Granny buys me are so old fashioned and babyish. Plus, if I had my own money, I could buy rhubarb-and-custard sweets every day from Aunt Marigold's store. They are my absolute favourites."

"I've got to go home for supper now, or Mum will be cross with me, but let's meet in the tree house later. We need to work out a money-making plan," said Poppy as she waved goodbye.

Chapter Four

Poppy was already waiting in the tree house when Honey arrived.

"Well, all we need is our own money and then we can do whatever we like, just like Daisy does," explained Poppy. "So we have to think of a way to make some extra pocket money."

Honey wasn't sure it was just about money, but she could see that Poppy was convinced this was the only thing stopping them from doing whatever they liked.

"We need to get jobs – that's what Daisy and her friends do. Daisy has her detective agency and a job at the stables, and she sometimes helps out at the Lighthouse Café too," Poppy went on.

"But what kind of jobs can we do?" asked Honey.

"That's what we need to work out," replied Poppy.

"I know – why don't we ask everyone we know in the Village whether they need any help with their work?" suggested Honey. "We could work at Saffron's shop, the Garden Centre and the Beauty Salon, or even clean cars for people."

"Good idea! Soon we'll have cool new bikes and lots of new clothes and we'll be able to do anything we like," grinned Poppy, thrilled that they'd come up with a solution to their problem.

"Poppy!" Mum called down the garden.

"It's time for your bath and then bed, darling. Which story would you like?"

Poppy thought it was much too early to go to bed – she was sure Daisy would still be hanging out with her friends in the Lighthouse Café. But the girls said goodnight to each other and arranged to meet the next day to put their plan into action.

Chapter Five

Early on Monday morning Poppy and
Honey set off on their money-making
mission. They decided to go and see Saffron
first. She always seemed to be so busy
designing and making all the clothes *and*
running the shop so the girls were sure she
would want some extra help.

"Morning, girls," called Saffron from
behind her sewing machine. "What can I do
for you?"

"Well, actually, we've come to help you,"

Poppy replied. "You see, me and Honey are trying to earn some extra pocket money because we really need new bikes and lots of other things, so we thought we could come and work for you."

"Well, girls, I know you are good workers and it would be lovely to have some help with the shop, but I'm afraid I just don't make enough money to pay anyone other than myself. Even if I could give you both jobs, I'd have to discuss everything with your mum, Poppy – and with Granny Bumble, Honey. Anyway, surely you're a bit too young to have jobs!" said Saffron.

Poppy and Honey were very downcast. They thanked Saffron and turned to leave. It would have been so cool to have a job at Saffron's shop. They really needed some extra pocket money – and fast!

"What now?" said Honey, looking to her friend for inspiration as they wandered along the river bank. "Maybe this *is* all about our age, Poppy."

"We can't give up yet! We'll find a way to earn some extra pocket money, I know we will. Let's go and see Sally Meadowsweet. There's always loads of work to do at the Garden Centre – I'm sure she'll have something we can do and I bet *she* can afford to pay us," said Poppy.

"What kind of stuff do you think she might want us to do?" asked Honey.

"Probably watering plants, weeding, picking flowers – easy stuff!" replied Poppy confidently.

Sally was busy sowing lettuce seeds when Poppy and Honey arrived.

"Hello, girls! What brings you here?" she asked, looking up from her work.

"Hi, Sally!" said Poppy cheerily. "We wondered whether you had any jobs that need doing here. We're trying to earn some money because we both need new bikes."

"What does your mum think about all this?" asked Sally. "And haven't you already got lovely bikes?"

"Our bikes are way too small for us and they're really babyish. I want to get a bike just like my cousin Daisy's," said Poppy.

"Well, I'm very impressed that you are prepared to earn money to get what you want, but the work here is much too heavy for you and I already have enough people working for me. I'm sorry," said Sally. "Anyway, you should save your energy for having fun and doing school work – you don't need to worry about money at your age!"

Poor Poppy was beginning to think that they would never be able to earn any money

– everyone was so concerned about
their age.

"OK, thanks, Sally. Bye, and good luck
with the planting," said Honey as they
headed for the exit.

As the girls walked back to Honeysuckle
Cottage, Poppy suddenly had another idea.

"You know there's a car boot sale at
Cornsilk Castle next Sunday? Well, maybe
we could sell some stuff there to make some
money," she suggested. "We could sell all our
old toys – everything that's too babyish, like
dolls and teddies. We could even sell our old
bikes. We won't need them any more if we're

going to buy new ones. It's the perfect answer to our problem."

Honey nodded. She wasn't completely sure if she wanted to give up all her old toys. Sometimes she still liked to play with them and she knew that Poppy did too, even if she wouldn't admit it. But she agreed to do it anyway – she wanted a new bike as much as Poppy did. Honey went back to her own house as Poppy went indoors.

Poppy looked around her pretty princess bedroom. It had glass doors opening onto the flowery garden and a princess bed with a muslin drape above it. All around were dolls, dressing-up clothes, teddies, toys and books. She opened the big toy cupboard to see whether there was anything in there that she might be able to sell at the car boot sale. There were soft toys, dolls, pretend cookers, a rocking horse and puzzles galore. All very babyish stuff – or so Poppy thought now.

Yes, all these can go! she thought boldly as she began to pull out things that she hadn't seen or played with for ages.

Poppy picked up her old teddy bear, Mr Bear-Bear, and put him on the 'to sell' pile. He had once been her favourite toy and she couldn't sleep unless she had him with her, but she was sure she didn't need him any more. She was far too grown up! Daisy didn't have soft toys on her bed. Next a full set of Colour Fairies figurines was put on the pile, then a fluffy white dog that moved his head as you pulled him along. Poppy couldn't resist trying him out one last time.

"Come on, Snowdrop," she called as he woofed and nodded across her bedroom floor. He made her think of the Christmas when she had been given him – she had been so excited when she unwrapped him!

Poppy finished by placing her beautiful wooden doll's house next to the 'to sell' pile.

Doll's houses are not for girls who hang out at the Lighthouse Café, Poppy thought. But a little voice in her head was saying, *Think how long it took Grandpa to make that doll's house. And think how thrilled you were when he brought it over and how often you still play with it!* Poppy didn't want to admit, even to herself, that it was still one of her favourite things.

Chapter Six

Meanwhile, over at Honeypot Cottage, Honey was going through all her toys.

Poor Honey was having a terrible time trying to decide what she could part with. So far she had only managed to put one jigsaw puzzle with a piece missing on her 'to sell' pile.

What if someone I know buys one of my lovely toys and I have to watch them enjoying it? That would be unbearable! she thought.

Just as she was agonizing over what else

she could part with to get a shiny new bike,
Granny Bumble popped her head round the
bedroom door.

"Having a good tidy up, are you?" she
asked. "You are a good girl!"

"Actually, Granny, I'm sorting out some
things for the car boot sale on Sunday.
Poppy wants me to choose some things to

sell – well, a lot of things – just old and babyish ones though. So we can make some extra pocket money to buy our new bikes," Honey explained. "Poppy thinks we should sell our old bikes there too."

Granny pursed her lips together – she only ever did this when she was really angry. "What new bikes?" she asked. "This is the first I've heard of it. What's wrong with the bikes you've got?"

"Poppy thinks our bikes are babyish – she wants a bike like her cousin Daisy's and I do too," Honey replied.

"I'll decide what goes in the sale. You still play with all these things, darling," said Granny. "You might get a little bit of money for your toys, but have you thought about what they are worth to you? If you and Poppy clear them all out, you'll need even more money to replace them with new things!"

Honey nodded. Granny Bumble was right. She and Poppy would have to think of another way of making some extra pocket money. Secretly she was relieved – she didn't want to get rid of her beloved toys at all, even for a shiny new bike.

"It's only a good idea to sell things when you are certain that that you will never need them again," Granny went on. "Poppy's mum will have the twins soon and I am sure that when they are old enough, they will want to play with all your old toys, and Poppy's too. If everyone turned their backs on things when they got older, I would be on the scrap heap too! Now clear up the mess you've made. I need to have a word with Lavender about all this. I bet Poppy hasn't told her what she's up to."

Granny Bumble loved Poppy, but sometimes she got carried away with things and this was one of those times. She lifted

the phone to call
Lavender Cotton.

"Hello, Fancy Hats,
Lavender speaking,"
said Poppy's mum.

"Hello,
Lavender, it's Granny
Bumble here. How are you
– not too tired, I hope?"

"Hi, Granny Bumble!
I'm fine, thanks – very
busy with the business,
but fine. I just want
these babies to be
born!" replied Poppy's
mum. "What can I do for you?"

"Well," began Granny Bumble, "I've just
found Honey pulling all her toys out of her
cupboard and trying to decide which ones
she can sell at the car boot sale. She still

plays with almost all of them. Honey tells me Poppy is doing the same and that it was Poppy who suggested it – apparently it's all to raise some money to buy new bikes. I'm really quite cross – it *is* very enterprising of the girls, but it's just not right. If they want new bikes, they'll have to wait until Christmas or their birthdays."

"Oh dear, I'm so sorry. Thank you for letting me know," replied Poppy's mum apologetically. "I completely agree with you – they mustn't sell their toys. I had no idea this was happening, although Poppy has been going on about wanting a new bike ever since she went to see her cousin in Camomile Cove last weekend. I'll go and sort this out with her right now."

"Poppy," Mum called as she walked into Poppy's bedroom, "I've just had Granny Bumble on the phone. She's told me all about your money-making plan and she's

very cross. So am I. On no account are you
to sell your precious things. These toys are
your whole childhood, Poppy. Me, Dad
and Grandpa have spent a lot of time and
money making or buying you all those
things. I would be very sad to see them go,
and I think you would be
too. And what if your
new brothers or sisters
want to play with their
big sister's old toys?"

Poppy nodded and a
huge tear rolled down
her cheek. It was a
tear of relief. There's
no way she could have
sold Mr Bear-Bear. And she really liked the
thought of the babies playing with her toys.
She was hoping they would look up to her
as much as she looked up to her older
cousins Daisy and Saffron.

Poppy realized she would have to think of another money-making plan in order to get her new bike.

Chapter Seven

Poppy's thoughts were interrupted by the phone ringing. It was Daisy!

"Hi, Daisy! How is the band?" asked Poppy. "Are you nearly ready for the barbecue?"

"Oh, Poppy, I've got loads to tell you," Daisy replied. "We've written a new song called *Good Luck Charm* and we need some backing singers. We wondered whether you and Honey would do it – you've both got such fab voices. You'll need to dress just like us and everything, so that the band has the right look. You should both come on the bike ride and the beach barbecue too. It's going to be really cool – please say you will!"

"Wow! Of course we will. Honey will be so excited – I can't wait to tell her," squealed Poppy.

"Can you both come over for a practice on Saturday? We'll need to work out what we're all going to wear, and when we've finished rehearsals, we can go for frappuccinos at the Lighthouse Café. Ask your mum if it's OK," said Daisy.

"I don't need to ask Mum," said Poppy. "She probably won't even notice – she's really tired out. I think it's because she is so massive!"

Poor Mum was

very upset. She couldn't believe what she was hearing. Her little princess was changing right before her eyes and she didn't like it one bit. Poppy was trying to grow up way too fast! Plus Mum hated being tired out and massive.

When Poppy put the phone down, she was so excited about everything that she didn't notice Mum was in the room and had heard the whole conversation. Then she saw that Mum looked cross and a bit tearful and she

knew she was in trouble. It was so annoying having to ask her parents before she could do anything fun. Poppy was sure Daisy didn't have to ask her mum and dad every time she wanted to do something.

"Poppy! What am I going to do with you? I take it that was Daisy? What is it that you don't need to ask me about?" asked Mum.

Poppy sat on the sofa next to Mum and told her all about the band, the bike ride and the beach barbecue. Then she tried to explain what she loved about Daisy's life and why she wanted that for herself.

"Mum, I want to be cool *now*. Me and Honey are really embarrassed by some of our stuff, especially our bikes. Daisy and her friends are so cool and they have so much fun. They've all got new bikes, they're in a band, they buy their own clothes and they're allowed to wear make-up," Poppy continued.

"But Daisy didn't do all those things when she was your age," said Mum. "It's brilliant that you and Daisy are friends, but I don't want you to grow up too fast. You'll have nothing left to look forward to if you do everything too soon. I'll talk to Dad and Granny Bumble about you and Honey going to this party, but I'm not making any promises."

Mum was very upset that Poppy wanted to be just like her cousin who was so much older. She liked things the way they were. She was also worried that older children would talk about things Poppy didn't understand and do things she was too young to do.

"What has happened to my baby girl?" asked Mum and put her arms around Poppy.

"Mum, I don't want to be your baby girl any more. I want to be cool, like Daisy. I want to be grown up. I wish people would stop treating me like a baby!" But Poppy still hugged Mum back.

Chapter Eight

The next day Granny Bumble took the girls up to the City on the train.

"Now, girls, what do you want to do?" she asked as they approached the City. "Would you like to go to the zoo?"

"Aw, I went there with Mum and Dad not long ago," said Honey. "Anyway, I don't like to see animals all squashed up in cages."

"Well, maybe the waxworks museum or the planetarium?" suggested Granny.

"I'd actually quite like to look at the shops," admitted Poppy.

"Me too," said Honey. "I've got a brilliant idea. We could go to the bicycle shop where Daisy got her bike. Just for a look!"

Granny laughed. The girls had obviously been planning this all along. "Oh, all right then," she smiled. "We'll go to Cycle Services and have a look at some bikes. Just a look, though. No new bikes until Christmas!"

When they walked into the shop, Poppy and Honey were completely mesmerized. It was absolutely enormous and had every sort of bike imaginable.

"Look, there's a bike just like Daisy's!" cried Poppy.

"That's too big for you, Poppy. And it'll still be too big at Christmas. You'll need a smaller one, like this," said Granny Bumble, pointing to a magnificent red shiny mountain bike called the Warrior Princess.

"Wow! I *love* it! And there's one in gold
for you, Honey," smiled Poppy. "But they're
so expensive!"

"Well, maybe if you girls save a bit of
money, Father Christmas might help with
the rest," suggested Granny Bumble.

Poppy and Honey were both rather
disappointed that they couldn't buy the bikes

there and then. Christmas seemed a long way off, and they needed the bikes for Daisy's end-of-term party in just over a week. They simply *had* to have them, whatever it took!

"That shop is awesome," said Poppy as they boarded the train home. "I've never wanted anything so much as that bike!"

Honey agreed. "Imagine how cool we would be at the barbecue on those bikes!"

Later that night, after Mum had read her a *Milly-Molly-Mandy* story, Poppy lay in bed thinking about the beautiful bike and trying to come up with some more money-making ideas. She chose to ignore the fact that Mum hadn't actually said they could go to the barbecue yet. She thought of all the different ways that people in the village earned money, hoping that it would give her a brainwave. She decided to make a list:

David Sage — Vet

Saffron Sage - fashion designer and shop owner

Mum - hat-maker

Aunt Marigold - general store owner

Sally Meadowsweet - garden centre owner

Lily Ann Peach - beautician + hairdresser

Granny Bumble - baker + teashop owner

Holly Mallow - school teacher + jewellery designer

Grandpa Mellow - newspaper editor

Farmer Meadowsweet - farmer

Dad - landscape gardener

When she had finished writing her list, Poppy had a sudden flash of inspiration. She realized that if they wanted to make

some extra pocket money, they would need to offer the villagers something they couldn't already get in Honeypot Hill.

On Wednesday morning Poppy and Honey met in the tree house and Poppy told her best friend about her flash of inspiration on the money-making front.

"We're good at *lots* of things – we just have to work out whether any of our talents can earn us some extra pocket money and get us the Warrior Princess bikes in time!" she explained. "What do you think we should do?"

"We could do face painting?" suggested Honey.

"Nah, too messy," Poppy replied.

"Or we could help old people with their housework or their shopping," said Honey.

"Maybe – let's write that down so we don't forget."

Poppy thought for a while. "We could walk people's dogs for them," she said.

"Although I can't really control big dogs," admitted Honey. "But I'm really good at Crazy Golf. We could design a course and charge people to use it."

"Sounds too tricky," said Poppy.

"Maybe I could do other children's homework for them for money," suggested Honey, who was very good at all school work.

Poppy looked shocked. "But then every jotter would look the same and that would be cheating, basically," she said impatiently. There had to be a better idea. "I know! When I was at the beach the other day, I saw a man giving donkey rides by the sea. We could tack up Twinkletoes and take him over there and charge people for rides."

"You're a genius! That's a great idea!" enthused Honey. "But how would we get him there?"

"I'll ask Dad to come with us and drive the horsebox, and he can help us with Twinkletoes and the money and everything. He always looks after me on Saturday mornings because that's when Mum makes up the bills for Fancy Hats. I'm sure he won't mind," said Poppy.

The girls were very pleased with themselves. They were absolutely convinced that this would earn them enough money to buy the beautiful bikes . . .

On Friday night, as Dad tucked Poppy in, she told him all about her latest money-making idea and asked him whether he would help her and Honey with the pony rides.

"Does Mum know about this?" Dad asked. "I know she's thinking about raising your pocket money slightly, but she didn't mention pony rides."

"Nope, she's too tired and busy with work, plus you always look after me on Saturdays. Me and Honey need to go to Camomile Cove tomorrow anyway to practise with the band," Poppy continued.

"What band?" asked Dad, feeling totally out of the loop that was Poppy's world.

"The Beach Babes. That's Daisy's band, and me and Honey are backing singers. We need new bikes for the barbecue beach party and bike ride next weekend so we've only got a week left to earn enough money to buy them. We're going to sing in the Battle of the Bands and then go for a bike ride and then go to the barbecue. It's going to be amazing!" Poppy explained.

Dad looked confused. He'd been working

so hard for the last couple of weeks that he didn't know anything about the band, the barbecue or even the bikes Poppy and Honey wanted so badly. "I'll discuss it with Mum," he said as he kissed Poppy goodnight and turned the light out.

Poppy could hear Mum and Dad talking in the next room. She sneaked out into the hall so that she could hear them better. She

knew she shouldn't listen in to other people's conversations, but she *had* to know what was going on. "At least she's trying to understand the value of money, Lavender. I think the pony-ride idea is very enterprising," said Dad.

"It's not about money, James," said Mum. "She's far too young to be hanging around with Daisy and her friends. I don't want her to go to the barbecue at all."

"But it's just a good weather thing. All children want to be more adventurous in the holidays. She's got all winter to sit indoors sewing and baking cookies. How about we say she can go on the condition that I go as well and keep an eye on her?" suggested Dad.

"But if we say she can go to the barbecue, that opens up the other issue about the new bike and all the other things she thinks she needs," said Mum. "And we'll have to discuss this with Granny Bumble — it involves Honey too."

"Let me deal with it – I'll ring her this evening. Maybe the girls will see how hard it is to earn money when they try themselves. They'll soon see that their old bikes are fine."

"I suppose they could try the pony thing – it might even make this whole money obsession go away," replied Mum.

Poppy was thrilled. She crept back to bed and fell asleep almost immediately, dreaming of riding through the woods on a gleaming new bike.

Chapter Nine

Saturday morning arrived bright and sunny. Poppy spent ages deciding what to wear. She eventually chose some blue and white checked pedal pushers, a white T-shirt and white lace espadrilles. She had one last look at herself in the mirror, put on some grape lip balm, and she was ready to go.

Dad and Poppy collected Honey and they all headed off to Riverside Stables together to tack up Twinkletoes and pick up David's horsebox.

"Come on, Twinkletoes, you've got a busy day ahead of you!" said Poppy.

The little chestnut pony obediently pitter-pattered his way out to the horsebox with Dad leading him by the reins. Then they all jumped into the front of the horsebox, strapped themselves in and started the half-hour journey to Camomile Cove.

Dad parked the horsebox near the beach and then helped Poppy and Honey take Twinkletoes to the promenade. The girls set up a sign to advertise the pony rides and settled down to wait for their first customer.

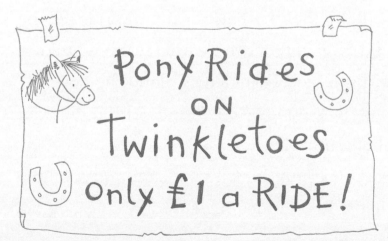

Pony Rides
ON
Twinkletoes
Only £1 a RIDE!

They didn't have to wait long. Very soon
a queue had formed and children were
begging their parents for a pony ride. Poppy
and Honey spent the whole morning taking
turns to lead Twinkletoes along the beach
and back again – each time with a different
child on his back.

"Don't you think Twinkletoes looks a little
tired?" said Honey after a rather big boy had
had a ride.

"He really does," agreed Dad. "Maybe we should give him a rest."

Poppy looked at all the coins in her tub and thought of the fabulous bicycle from the city, then she looked at her precious little pony. She didn't think they had made enough money yet and really wanted to carry on doing pony rides until they had some more, but deep down she knew that Twinkletoes had had enough and they would have to stop.

"Just one more ride," Poppy declared. She was getting tired too – it was hard work, especially in the sunshine. "Then we can go over to Daisy's for the rehearsal. She's expecting us at one o'clock."

After the last pony ride, Poppy, Honey and Dad gathered all their stuff together and led Twinkletoes over to Shellbay House. He could graze in the garden until they were ready to go home – there was lots of yummy green grass for him to munch on there. Dad went to have coffee with Delphi and Daniel, and Poppy and Honey joined the older girls

for the band rehearsal in the summer house. Honey's eyes nearly popped out of her head when she saw it. Poppy hadn't been exaggerating – it was so cool.

"Hi, girls!" said Daisy, and then she introduced Honey to Lily and Rose. "How did the pony rides go?"

"Really well. We've made lots of money for our bike fund – we want to get new ones for the bike ride next weekend!" said Poppy. "We're saving up just like you did."

"Wow, that sounds great, but don't work too hard," Daisy replied, concerned for the younger girls. "You must have time for fun too. I didn't have a job at your age, and we only opened up the detective agency a year ago."

"Let's start rehearsals," said Lily as she passed round song sheets and then told Poppy and Honey when to come in with their tambourines, triangles and 'doo-bi-doo-ahs'.

The Beach Babes sounded pretty good
– even better now that they had backing
singers! The rehearsal was excellent fun –
all the girls were so excited about
performing *Good Luck Charm* in front
of an audience.

"Well done, everyone," said Daisy when
they were finished. "That was fab! We
absolutely *have* to win the Battle of the
Bands next week – the boys can't be
better than us!"

Poppy and Honey smiled proudly at each
other – they felt so grown up.

"We need to work out what we're all
going to wear before you girls go back to
Honeypot Hill. We were thinking of going
for a low-key, cool kind of look – smocks,
shorts, flip-flops, that sort of thing. Does
that sound OK?" Daisy asked the two
younger girls.

"That sounds great," replied Poppy

confidently, although she didn't really know
what Daisy meant and she was pretty sure
none of her clothes would be quite right. She
had a week to sort the problem out.

"The song sounded very funky, girls," said
Dad as he popped his head round the door
of the summer house. "I'm going to have to
take your two backing singers away though.
We should get Twinkletoes home – he's had
a busy day."

Poppy and Honey said goodbye to the
older girls. They went with Dad to collect
Twinkletoes from his grazing post in the
corner of Daisy's garden, led him back
to the horsebox and then set off for
Honeypot Hill.

They put Twinkletoes to bed in his cosy
little stable, gave him a fresh net of hay and
kissed him goodbye. Then they walked back
to Honeysuckle Cottage.

As soon as they got back, the girls dashed

off to Poppy's room to count their day's
earnings. They had made quite a bit of extra
pocket money but nowhere near enough for
the shiny new bikes. They wanted the bikes
more than ever after their trip to Camomile
Cove, but they both agreed that they
couldn't do pony rides again – Twinkletoes

needed a rest. Time was running out: they had less than a week left to earn enough money . . .

Chapter Ten

On Sunday Grandpa was looking after
Poppy and Honey while everyone else was
at the car boot sale. While they were sitting
in his conservatory looking out over his
beautiful garden, Poppy came up with a new
and brilliant money-making idea.

"Grandpa, you know how you always
have to throw quite a lot of your home-
grown fruit and vegetables on the compost
heap because you have too much?" Poppy
began. "Well, don't you think it would be

better to sell them rather than to waste them? Me and Honey could sell them for you."

Honey's face lit up. "Selling vegetables! That's a perfect plan – we'll definitely have new bikes in time!"

"You're right. It is a shame to waste them, especially since I put so much effort into growing them," said Grandpa. "I'd be happy for you to sell them as long as you give me some of your earnings so that I can buy seeds for my next crop."

"OK then, it's a deal," smiled Poppy as she shook Grandpa's hand.

"What will we put them in?" asked Honey.

"I've got an old wooden wheelbarrow somewhere in the shed," said Grandpa. The girls went to have a look. The wheelbarrow was very muddy, so they decided to hose it down before their produce went in. When it

was clean and dry, the girls loaded the
wheelbarrow up with tomatoes, peapods
and broad beans. Some of the root
vegetables had to be dug out of the ground
first. It was very hard work!

"Poppy, do you think we should make a
price list?" asked Honey.

Poppy had never noticed fruit and
vegetable prices before, even though she

knew exactly how much a chocolate-fudge sundae at Bumble Bee's Teashop cost.

"Let's just make it up as we go along," said Poppy. "I'm sure that will be fine."

"That all looks great, girls – you'll be brilliant vegetable sellers!" said Grandpa. "Now, it's getting late. You should go home for supper and you can start selling in the morning. I'll look after your produce for you overnight."

"Thanks, see you tomorrow!" chorused the girls.

In the morning Poppy and Honey dressed for work. They tied their hair back and tucked their jeans into their flowery wellies. Then they went to pick up the veggie-barrow from Grandpa's house. They decided that the best way to sell their fruit and vegetables was to simply knock on doors around the Village and see whether people wanted to buy any.

Most people bought two or three types of vegetables. Grandpa had a very good reputation for gardening. But because Poppy and Honey had never done anything like this before, the prices they charged were much too low. Everyone in Honeypot Hill seemed to have heard about the bargain organic fruit and vegetables, and soon people were coming to them and a queue formed in front of the wheelbarrow.

Grandpa's organic veg for Sale

"You know how people always buy lettuce with tomatoes?" said Honey. "Why don't we do a special price for people who take both? And we could do a carrot and leek special for soups."

"That's a great idea!" enthused Poppy.

Just as they were congratulating themselves on how good they were at making money and how much they were learning, Aunt Marigold appeared in a ball of orange fury.

"You girls! I can't keep up with you. If I'd known you'd be giving away vegetables practically for free, I'd never have bought so many at market this morning. All my stock is going to go bad. It would have been nice of you to let me know you were going to be doing this!" said Aunt Marigold crossly.

Poppy and Honey blushed. They hadn't meant to upset anyone, they just wanted to earn some extra pocket money!

"We're so sorry, Aunt Marigold," they chorused. "We didn't mean to spoil your sales!"

"We have an unspoken rule here in the village that no one will spoil another person's trade by competing with them," explained Aunt Marigold. "If I set up a teashop, your granny wouldn't be very pleased, would she, Honey? And if I started making pretty hats, Poppy, *your* mum wouldn't like it."

The girls nodded. They could see what she meant. They decided to take a break and think about what to do next. They left their wheelbarrow, which was still half-full of fruit and vegetables, near the door of Bumble Bee's Teashop and went in for an ice-cream sundae.

While Poppy and Honey were sitting in the teashop with their backs to the window, Farmer Meadowsweet's prize piglet, Pippa, came ambling merrily along the Main Street. This was not unusual. She often escaped and had a little nose about the Village before someone called the farmer and he came to collect her. Pippa thought today was her lucky day when she smelled fresh vegetables in the air. She was starving! The hungry little piglet made a bee-line for the wheelbarrow. She nuzzled into it, grunted triumphantly and tore into the remaining produce. In her excitement she upset the barrow and all the vegetables tumbled into the street and began rolling down towards the River Swan.

Poppy and Honey heard a noise and
turned round to check on their wheelbarrow.

"*Oh no!*" shrieked Poppy. "It's Pippa. She's
been at our barrow!"

They rushed outside to see what they
could do, and the piglet, realizing she was
in trouble, took flight, trotting along the
Main Street as fast as her porky little body
would allow. Poppy started to chase her,
while Honey ran towards the river to gather
up the escaped vegetables. Poppy slipped on
an onion skin as she saw Pippa disappearing
into the distance. Honey went over to help
and slipped on another onion skin, landing
in a heap right next to Poppy!

"I don't think this is working out," moaned Honey.

"Me neither. I never ever want to see another vegetable!" said Poppy, and they decided it was time to come up with yet another money-making idea.

Back at Honeysuckle Cottage Poppy and Honey made headings in their notebooks and talked about new ways they could make some extra pocket money. While they were doing this, Mum came to see what they were up to.

"Oh, girls! Are you *still* obsessed with these bikes? I can't understand what's wrong with the ones you've got. You were perfectly happy

with them two weeks ago! Why don't you go and play on your scooters like you used to, or paint pebbles, rather than thinking about money all the time?" she suggested.

Poppy's eyes lit up. "Painted pebbles! What a great idea! Saffron could sell them in her shop."

Honey shook her head. "Each pebble takes about two days to make, with the varnish and everything. Plus it wouldn't be fun any more if we had to make lots of them in a rush," she said. "Maybe your mum is right. We should just stop thinking about making money. We're never going to have enough for the bikes in time anyway. And your mum and my granny haven't exactly said that we can go to the barbecue yet. And what's the point of the bikes if we can't go to the barbecue?"

Poppy was pretty sure Dad had nearly persuaded Mum that she could go, but she was fed up thinking about money all the time too.

The girls went to Poppy's bedroom to play for a bit before supper. While they flicked through some books and magazines together, Poppy started to hum the tune of *Good Luck Charm*. Honey joined in too.

"Honey, take a hairbrush and pretend it's a microphone. Let's practise our backing vocals. Here – have some of the grape lip balm that Daisy gave me!"

The girls looked into the mirror and began to sing and dance around, giggling and flicking their hair as they pretended to be pop stars

and imagined a huge crowd dancing and singing along to their music!

"*Do-bi-doo-ahh, Good Luck Charm, do-bi-doo*," they sang in harmony.

Then they tried on some of Mum's high heels and started to sing into Poppy's karaoke machine.

"You know what?" said Poppy to Honey. "We have to go to the barbecue on new bikes and sing in the band. I really, really want to."

"Me too, more than anything!" admitted Honey. "Imagine being up on stage with Daisy's friends. It would be so cool – probably the best thing in the world ever!"

"We still need to earn more money! How are we ever going to get the right idea?" said Poppy.

As the girls sat at Poppy's dressing table, trying different hairstyles and despairing of ever having enough money for the

wonderful new bikes, Poppy
spotted the lovely perfume
bottle filled with petal perfume
and tied with a ribbon that
Honey had given her for her
birthday. She dabbed some on
her wrists and put her wrist up
to her nose.

"I've got it!" she exclaimed.
"Really, really. This is the one.
What about becoming perfume-
makers? We need lots of petals,
lots of ribbons and lots of pretty
glass bottles."

"Perfect!" smiled Honey.
"If only we'd thought of that
sooner."

Chapter Eleven

The girls got started on the perfume early the next morning. They found lots of glass bottles in Granny Bumble's outhouse, which she had collected for 'useful purposes'. She agreed that they could have the bottles for free. Saffron gave them ends of rolls from her ribbons – they were too short for her to sell, but perfect for Poppy and Honey's purposes – and Grandpa let them collect lots of petals in his garden.

They mixed the petals with pure spring

water and poured the perfume into the pretty bottles. They decided to call it Princess Petals, and before long they were ready to start selling it.

"Where would be the best place to sell perfume?" Poppy wondered as they made a pretty label for each bottle:

princess Petals
a special Perfume
by
Poppy & Honey

"I think just outside the Beehive Beauty Salon – ladies who like beauty treatments will like to smell nice too," said Honey sensibly. "But we'll have to ask Lily Ann whether she minds – remember what happened with Aunt Marigold and the vegetables!"

"I will recommend Princess Petals to everyone who comes into the Beehive Beauty Salon," said Lily Ann Peach kindly when the girls asked her permission to set up their stall.

They took an old folding table, covered it with a pale pink cloth and put a vase of flowers on top. The perfume-selling went very smoothly indeed and soon they had sold out.

Later that day, when they got back to Poppy's cottage, they counted all their money and realized that they'd made quite a lot from all the ideas they'd had over the past week.

"Well done, girls," said Mum. "You've been very imaginative and hard-working!"

"I know, but we still don't have enough for the bikes," Poppy sighed. "Even if we make some more perfume and work really hard for the rest of the week, we'll never have enough money in time for the barbecue."

"Anyway, Dad and I haven't actually said yes yet, have we?" said Mum.

"Oh, please, Mum. We have to go. Daisy and the Beach Babes need us!" pleaded Poppy.

"I'll talk to your father again, and to your granny, Honey," promised Mum. "Why don't you two go and visit Twinkletoes. You've not had much time for him this week, what with all your money-making ideas. I expect he's missing you."

"That's a good idea," agreed Honey.

"I know," said Poppy, "why don't we give him a proper pampering session to say thank you for working so hard for us last weekend. We're never going to have enough money for the bikes but we do have enough to buy Twinks a gorgeous halter and a new grooming kit. Mum, can you take us to Ned's?"

Mum looked on proudly. *Imagine thinking of Twinkletoes before themselves after all their hard work*, she thought.

Mum took them to Ned's the next day and they bought a new grooming kit, a sparkly halter and a fleecy blanket. As they were waiting for the train home, they spotted Daisy, Lily and Rose.

"Hi, Daisy!" Poppy called.

"Hi, girls! What are you doing in

Camomile Cove today – you're a bit early
for the barbecue, aren't you?" smiled Daisy.

"Oh, we've just been to Ned's. Me and
Honey decided to spend all the extra pocket
money we earned on some treats for
Twinkletoes. We thought we'd spend it on
him as we're never going to have enough
money for new bikes in time for the

barbecue – anyway, I don't think Mum, Dad and Granny Bumble are going to let us come – Mum thinks we're too young *and* we haven't got the right bikes or clothes or anything," explained Poppy. "But I hope it all goes well and I *really* hope you beat Caves 'n' Rocks!"

"Oh, Poppy!" said Daisy. "You don't need to have fancy bikes to hang out with us or be in our band. Come anyway. We'll lend you clothes. We need your lovely singing voices to win the competition!"

"Mum, *can* we go?" asked Poppy quietly.

"I'll see what Dad and Granny Bumble think," said Mum.

When they got back to Honeypot Hill, Poppy and Honey raced off to see Twinkletoes and give him his treats. He was going to look gorgeous. Dad met Mum at the station and drove her home – she found it very tiring to walk far because of her big baby bump. On the way home Mum told Dad how impressed she was with Poppy and Honey.

"You know, I think I was wrong about those girls," she admitted. "I know they're desperate to go to the barbecue and I really wasn't happy about it even if you went too, but they've been so clever and determined about their bike money. I think they've realized that money doesn't grow on trees. They deserve a treat. I think we should let them go as long as you keep an eye on them."

"They'll be so happy," Dad replied. "And I agree with you: they have really grown up in the last couple of weeks. I can't wait to see them perform – I've heard them practising and they sounded pretty good!"

Chapter Twelve

On the morning of the barbecue Poppy woke up with a heavy heart. She had pretty much given up hope of going because Mum and Dad hadn't said anything more about it and she didn't think it wise to pester them any more!

I just wish tomorrow would come so I can stop thinking about what I am missing out on today, she thought. She looked at her karaoke machine longingly. *Just think – I was almost a pop star!*

Poppy went down for breakfast feeling very downcast. She sat at the table and looked into her empty bowl.

"Morning, darling," said Mum. "Have you noticed anything different in here?"

Poppy looked up. She had no idea what Mum was talking about, until she saw the gleaming red Warrior Princess bike, tied with a huge red satin ribbon, propped up against

the back door. She thought she was dreaming and almost choked with surprise and delight when she saw it.

"Is that for me?" she squealed.

"Of course it is, darling!" said Mum, taking a photograph of Poppy's ecstatic expression. "We bought it with the money we made at the car boot sale."

Poppy ran to hug Mum and Dad. "Thank you! Thank you so much! But what about Honey?"

"Honey has one too," Mum reassured her. "Granny Bumble ordered the gold Warrior Princess for her."

"Does this mean we can go to the barbecue?"

"Yes, but Dad is coming with you," explained Mum. "I'd love to come, but—" She looked down to her tummy. "I'll be there for the Beach Babes' performance though!"

"You are the best fairy godmother in the

entire world!" said Poppy. "And the biggest!"

Mum and Dad laughed.

"We can't disappoint our little Pocket Money Princess, can we?" said Mum. "Especially when she behaves like such a good little princess!"

Poppy and Honey put on their new helmets and practised cycling up and down the street. By lunch time they were ready to head off to Camomile Cove.

"Dad, do you have to cycle with us?" asked Poppy. "It's just – well, your bike's a bit, you know—"

"A bit past it? I know it is, Poppy, but that's because *you* get all the treats around here! Oh, all right then. I'll cycle well behind you!" laughed Dad.

When they reached the cove, the party was in full swing on the beach and in the nearby grassy field. Daisy saw Poppy and Honey and came running over to them.

"You've made it! Thank goodness. The song sounds much better with you two – we'll definitely win!"

Poppy and Honey smiled proudly. Daisy gave them pretty cotton gypsy blouses and cut-off jeans to wear and they looked just like the older girls. She also tied scarves round their heads and gave them some strawberry lip balm.

"Wow!" said Lily as she joined them. "Look at your bikes. They're so cool!"

Poppy and Honey beamed with pride – they were cool at last!

"Come on, you lot," called Rose. "The Beach Babes are on!"

Poppy and Honey climbed onto the makeshift platform and took their places at the back. Daisy started them off by making an introduction: "We are the Beach Babes and we're going to sing *Good Luck Charm*!"

Poppy and Honey concentrated really

hard and waited for their cues. Even they could hear that the song sounded wonderful – the crowd loved it. When they were finished, everyone screamed: "Again!" "More!" So they performed it one more time.

Even though the boys' band was great, the screams were louder for the Beach Babes and they won the vote. They could see that even Lilac Farrington and all her super-cool friends were screaming their support.

At the end of the show Daisy got back on the stage and asked the crowd to donate what they could to charity in the bins provided. Honey and Poppy put in the money they had left over from their earnings after buying Twinkletoes' presents and felt great about it.

"Imagine giving our very *own* money to charity. We're so grown up – just like Daisy and her friends!" said Honey, adjusting her head scarf.

"Now we're all going to cycle through the woods before we have the barbecue!" announced Daisy. "Come on, Warrior Princesses. Follow us!"

Poppy suddenly noticed that Lilac

Farrington, the coolest girl at Smuggler's
Cove, was on an old bike with a basket on
the front.

*Maybe having the smartest bike isn't as
important as taking part,* thought Poppy. *But I
do love my new bike so much.*

She didn't even notice her dad cycling at
the edge of the crowd of children. She was so
happy – all their hard work had paid off and
now they were hanging around with Daisy
and her friends. It felt great, but she realized
that it wasn't earning money that made her
feel so good, it was learning that she couldn't
just have anything she wanted. She loved her

bike all the more because she had worked so hard for it – even if it had been a gift in the end.

Then Poppy caught sight of Dad cycling through the trees. She felt lucky to have parents who cared about her so much.

"How's it going, Pocket Money Princess?" called Dad.

"Everything is amazing," grinned Poppy as she zoomed past on her beautiful new bike. "But making money is a lot harder than I imagined! I think I'll leave that to you and Mum for a little while longer."

THE END